3 Pandas Planting

by **Megan Halsey**

Marshall Cavendish Children

Text and illustrations copyright © 1994 by Megan Halsey
Originally published by Bradbury Press, 1994
First Marshall Cavendish paperback edition, 2011

Marshall Cavendish Corporation
99 White Plains Road, Tarrytown, NY 10591
www.marshallcavendish.us/kids

Library of Congress Cataloging-in-Publication Data
Halsey, Megan.
3 pandas planting / by Megan Halsey. — 1st Marshall Cavendish pbk. ed.
p. cm.
ISBN 978-0-7614-5844-9
1. Counting—Juvenile literature. 2. Animals—Juvenile literature.
3. Ecology—Juvenile literature. I. Title. II. Title: Three pandas planting.
QA113.H36 2011   640—dc22   2010017164

The illustrations are rendered in gouache and gesso, with pen-and-ink line
work, and colored pencil and pastels used for shading and detail.

Book design by Vera Soki
Editor: Nathalie Le Du

Printed in China (E)
1 3 5 6 4 2

This book is dedicated to
all the friends of the earth.

12 Crocodiles

We're carpooling.

11 Tigers

We turn off our faucets.

10 Otters

We're organized:
bottles in one bin, trash in another.

9 Turtles

We take our cans home.

8 Condors

We're collecting litter!

We're changing light bulbs to save electricity.

7 Chimps

6 Bears

We bundle our newspapers for recycling.

We're learning about recycling.

5 Leopards

4 Rhinos

We use rechargeable batteries.

We plant trees.

3 Pandas

2 Whales

We're watching for polluters.

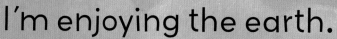

I'm enjoying the earth.

1 Elephant

Family Tips for Taking Care of the Earth

Save Energy

- Carpool, walk, ride a bike, or take a bus or train, so there will be fewer vehicles on the road polluting the air with exhaust fumes.
- Use energy-saving fluorescent light bulbs and turn off the lights after you leave a room, so less electricity is used and less carbon pollutes our air.
- Learn more about saving energy at:
    - The U.S. Department of Energy: www.eia.doe.gov/kids and www.eere.energy.gov/kids
    - The Environmental Protection Agency: www.epa.gov/climatechange/emissions/ind_calculator2.html

Keep the Air Clean

- Plant trees! Trees help keep the air clean by producing oxygen and absorbing pollution.
- "Buy local." Buying food grown locally means trucks carrying food from faraway places won't have to drive long distances, polluting the air with exhaust fumes.
- Learn more about keeping the air clean at:
  - The Arbor Day Foundation: www.arborday.org/explore/families
  - The Environmental Defense Fund: www.fightglobalwarming.com/documents/5204_fgwdownloadkids.pdf

Conserve Water

- Use water sparingly when brushing teeth or washing dishes.
- Check the house for leaky faucets because they contribute to water loss.
- Create a rain barrel to catch rain for watering plants instead of using water from a faucet.
- Learn more about conserving water at the Environmental Protection Agency: www.epa.gov/watersense/kids

Recycle

- Sort and recycle paper, glass, aluminum, and plastic products since they decompose slowly and can harm the earth.
- Buy plastic items that have the numbers 1 and 2 on them, since they can be recycled easily.
- Learn about your town's recycling program and the ways in which you can participate.
- Take recyclables home with you if you are out where there are no recycling bins.
- Learn more about recycling at:
    - Earth911.com: www.earth911.com/recycling/glass/video-how-glass-gets-recycled
    - America Recycles Day: www.americarecyclesday.org

Reduce and Reuse

- Reuse old shopping bags or buy fabric reusable ones. By doing so, fewer trees will be cut down to make paper bags.
- Recycle trash by donating or selling old clothes, toys, and other unwanted items instead of throwing them away.
- Compost food scraps and lawn trimmings instead of dropping them in the garbage.
- Buy items made from recycled paper so fewer trees will be cut down.
- Learn more about reducing and reusing at the Environmental Protection Agency: www.epa.gov/recyclecity

Fun Earth Events

World Water Day is March 22nd: www.unwater.org/worldwaterday

Earth Day is April 22nd: www.epa.gov/earthday and www.earthday.org

Arbor Day is recognized on different days according to your state's climate. Most states hold events at the end of April: www.arborday.org

World Environment Day is June 5th: www.unep.org

America Recycles Day is November 15th: www.americarecyclesday.org

Atlanta-Fulton Public Library